The Night of Courage

Danielle Star

Scholastic Inc.

Copyright © 2016 by Atlantyca Dreamfarm s.r.l., Via Leopardi 8, 20123 Milan, Italy. International Rights © Atlantyca S.p.A. English translation © 2018 by Atlantyca S.p.A.

The publisher does not have any control over and does not assume any responsibility for author or third-party websites or their content.

All names, characters, and related indicia contained in this book are the copyright and exclusive license of Atlantyca S.p.A. in their original version. The translated and/or adapted versions are the property of Atlantyca S.p.A. All rights reserved.

Published by Scholastic Inc., *Publishers since 1920,* 557 Broadway, New York, NY 10012. SCHOLASTIC and associated logos are trademarks and/or registered trademarks of Scholastic Inc.

No part of this publication may be reproduced, stored in a retrieval system, or transmitted in any form or by any means, electronic, mechanical, photocopying, recording, or otherwise without written permission of the copyright holder. For information regarding permission, please contact: Atlantyca S.p.A., Via Leopardi 8, 20123 Milan, Italy; e-mail foreignrights@atlantyca.it, www.atlantyca.com.

This book is a work of fiction. Names, characters, places, and incidents are either the product of the author's imagination or are used fictitiously, and any resemblance to actual persons, living or dead, business establishments, events, or locales is entirely coincidental.

ISBN 978-1-338-15178-7

Text by Danielle Star
Original title *La notte del coraggio*
Editorial cooperation by Lucia Vaccarino
Illustrations by Igor Chimisso (layout), Miriam Gambino (clean up), and Alessandra Bracaglia (colors)
Graphics by Danielle Stern

Special thanks to Tiffany Colón
Translated by Chris Turner
Interior design by Baily Crawford

10 9 8 7 6 5 4 3 2 1   18 19 20 21 22

Printed in the U.S.A.   40
First printing 2018

Contents

Imagine a magical land wrapped in golden light. A planet in a distant galaxy beyond the known stars. This enchanted place is known as Aura, and it is very special. For Aura is home to the pegasus, a winged horse with a colorful mane and coat.

The pegasuses of Aura come from four ancient island realms that lie within Aura's enchanted oceans: the Winter Realm of Amethyst Island, the Spring Realm of Emerald Island, the Day Realm of Ruby Island, and the Night Realm of Sapphire Island.

A selected number from each realm are born with a symbol on their wings and a hidden magical power. These are the Melowies.

When their magic beckons them in a dream, all Melowies leave their island homes to answer the call. They must attend school at the Castle of Destiny, a legendary castle hidden in a sea of clouds, where they will learn all about their hidden powers. Destiny is a place where friendships are born, where Melowies find their courage, and where they discover the true magic inside themselves!

Map of Aura

Map of the Castle of Destiny

Meet the Melowies

Cleo

Her realm: unknown
Her personality: impulsive and loyal
Her passion: writing
Her gift: something mysterious . . .

Electra

Her realm: Day
Her personality: boisterous and bubbly
Her passion: fashion
Her gift: the Power of Light

Maya

Her realm: **Spring**

Her personality: **shy and sweet**

Her passion: **cooking**

Her gift: **the Power of Heat**

Cora

Her realm: **Winter**

Her personality: **proud and sincere**

Her passion: **ice-skating**

Her gift: **the Power of Cold**

Selena

Her realm: **Night**

Her personality: **deep and sensitive**

Her passion: **music**

Her gift: **the Power of Darkness**

1
A Strange New Teacher

The sun had been up for quite some time at the Castle of Destiny. The first-year students were already awake and in their classroom, waiting for their new teacher.

Suddenly, the door opened and a tornado swept in and swirled to the front of the classroom. Clouds of papers, pencils, and books flew up into the air behind it. The tornado settled into a Melowy wearing a leather jacket and cowboy hat that looked about a hundred years old. She also wore a few belts around her waist. The girls in the front row quickly noticed that her breath wasn't as fresh as it could be.

It was *her*, every student's worst nightmare, the defense techniques teacher, Ms. Ariadne. The students whispered nervously to one another.

"Silence!" the teacher yelled. The whispering instantly stopped. "As you may already know, my name is Ms. Ariadne. I have been given the impossible task of teaching you weaklings how to defend yourselves. Let's not waste any time. Who can tell me why we study defense techniques?"

None of the Melowies dared to speak.

"Has a cat got all your tongues?"

Electra bravely raised her hoof and tried to answer. "To learn how to survive?"

"Very good, dear. What is your name?" Ms. Ariadne asked.

"Electra."

"So, as Rebecca here says, you will learn survival skills in this class. Though, very few of you are likely to actually survive." Ms.

Ariadne giggled to herself, as if the idea of the Melowies being unable to survive was funny.

"Excuse me." The brave Melowy with the fiery red mane dared to speak again. "My name is not Rebecca. It's Electra."

"You are probably right, Henrietta, but I should tell you all right now that I can never remember names. Anyway, what does the word *survival* mean to you weaklings?"

"How dare she call us weak!" Cora whispered to Maya, who was sitting in front of her. The five roommates were all sitting together. The classroom was huge; its walls were covered with books and tall windows that overlooked a sea of clouds that surrounded the Castle of Destiny.

"I don't like this teacher very much

already," Cleo whispered. Her friends all turned toward her to hear what she would say next.

Cleo had a mysterious past. She was found on the front steps of the castle when she was a baby, and no one had any idea who her parents were or what realm she came from. She always had something interesting to say, and she always had the courage to say it, even if her opinion was different from everyone else's.

"Well," Cleo began, "survival means staying alive after doing something dangerous. Like—"

"Oh, I know! Like going a whole week without listening to music!" Selena interrupted.

The teacher opened her mouth and closed it again. Her face scrunched up like she had just tasted a spoonful of terrible medicine. "What is your name, dear?"

"Selena."

"Well, Irena, if that's what you believe, your ideas are going to get a little shaken up here. Can anyone else give me the definition of the word *survival*?"

"It means staying alive after going to the dentist?" Maya suggested shyly.

"Or after eating a whole plate of cauliflower!" Electra added.

"My dear, young, silly girls. I think the time has

come for you all to learn the true meaning of the word *survival*. Please stand up and form a line. I am now going to take you into the Neon Forest for a survival challenge that will teach you many skills. For example, you will learn how to build shelter for the night, how to light a fire, and which plants you can and can't eat. Just remember, you won't have a lot of time to complete the challenge. You must all be back at your camp by ten o'clock tomorrow morning. Alive, if you can manage that." The teacher chuckled to herself, but no one else in the room cracked a smile.

"Excuse me, but I don't have a watch. Will one be given to us?" said Electra.

"Why would you need a watch? My dear, don't you ever look at the sun? It's the best clock there is! You should know that, since you are from the Day Realm." She turned to face the rest of the class. "The school will provide you with these rather frilly backpacks, which contain everything you will need to survive this challenge."

She shook her head slightly, and the braid of her hair jiggled. Suddenly, a flash of pink lights filled the room, and a backpack appeared on the shoulders of each Melowy. They perfectly matched each girl's coat and wings!

"Oh, I love accessories!" Cora whispered

to Electra, admiring her icy-blue backpack. "This one looks so good on me."

"This teacher is really strange. She can't remember anyone's name, but somehow she knows that I am from the Day Realm."

"You will be broken into groups of six," Ms. Ariadne said.

Cora, Electra, Maya, Cleo, and Selena all looked at one another. "I hope she doesn't break us up!" Maya whispered.

"There already seems to be a group of five here. Who would like to join this bunch?" the teacher asked.

"I will," came a cold voice from the back of the room.

"Eris?!" Electra gasped, turning to her friends.

"Why on earth would she want to join us?" Selena whispered, trying to make sure the teacher didn't hear her. "She doesn't like us! Ever since she poured paint all over me in the middle of the school musical, I don't like her very much, either."

"Maybe she is trying to change and get to know us better," Electra said. She tried to see the best in everyone and everything. "With her icy personality, it must be really hard for her to make new friends."

"Well, I don't trust her, but maybe we can give her a chance," Cleo suggested.

"If Eris wants to try to be friends with us, that's okay with me," Maya agreed. She was a very sensitive Melowy, and she always wanted to help others.

"It's okay with us, too," the others echoed.

"What are you girls mumbling about over there?" Ms. Ariadne interrupted. "Kindly be quiet!"

Cora turned toward the teacher and, suddenly, Ms. Ariadne was gone. She was swallowed up by a tangle of shadows and branches.

The classroom had disappeared, and they were now standing in the middle of a thick forest.

2
Invisible Ink

The Castle of Destiny was probably the only place where you could be standing in a classroom one moment and be magically transported to a forest full of trees the next.

"I'm not scared . . . I'm not scared . . . I'm not scared . . . ," Maya kept repeating to herself. "Yes, I am! I'm terrified. There are probably poisonous insects, snakes, and plants here."

"Have they given us anything to protect

ourselves from snakes?" Cleo asked, searching in her backpack. Inside she found a change of clothes, a towel, a toothbrush, a tube of toothpaste, bandages, gauze, a ball of string, a pair of scissors, a flashlight, a cooking pot, some cutlery, and a sealed envelope. "Nope, not a thing for snakes," Cleo said, looking disappointed. "They gave us everything we need for a great sleepover, but nothing to protect us from snakes."

"Have they given us anything to scare off the zombies?" Electra joked, opening her golden backpack, which contained all the same items. "Maybe there is something useful in the envelope," she said, opening it up. The piece of paper inside was completely blank. Her friends opened theirs to find the same thing.

"It looks like it's going to get dark soon," said Maya with a shiver. "Time must be different here." She turned on her flashlight to make sure it worked.

The peach glow of the sunset was casting long shadows in the forest. The trees were blowing in the wind, making strange and scary sounds.

"Hey, you guys, look!" Maya shouted. "Some writing has appeared on my piece of paper!" Maya turned her flashlight toward the paper to get a better look, and the heat of the light made letters appear.

"Ms. Ariadne must have used lemon juice to write this," said Eris, who had been silent until then. "It's called invisible ink."

They huddled around the sheet of paper to read. It was instructions on how to build a shelter using branches and leaves. At the bottom of the page, in bold letters, was

the line: *The biggest mistake is being afraid to make mistakes.*

"I wonder what she means by that," Cora whispered.

"I have a feeling we'll find out eventually," Cleo said. "Come on. Let's see where this trail leads."

They zipped up their backpacks and followed the trail ahead of them. It wound its way through the forest like a silk ribbon.

The Melowies had heard stories of how magical the Neon Forest was. All the stories were true! The plants and trees changed colors as the light changed. As the sun set, the plants began to glow a brilliant blue. There were clusters of flowers that went from pink to scarlet to deep purple to pink again.

All around the girls, tiny insects with glowing antennae floated around, tracing out circles of orange lights.

"This place is beautiful!" exclaimed

Selena, who had always felt comfortable with the magic of the night.

Suddenly, they could hear the babbling of a brook in the distance. Cora immediately flew over to it.

"There's nothing better than an icy-cold dip to help you relax! All this walking is making me sweat!" She lowered herself into the water, which sparkled with emerald-green rings when she moved. "Come on, guys, the water's just fine!"

Maya and Selena slowly walked toward the water and dipped in their hooves. "It's freezing!" they both cried.

"When you all are finished wasting valuable time, we're going to have to find a good place to build our shelter," Eris interrupted, reminding them of their task.

"How about right over there?" Electra pointed to a clearing surrounded by tall trees

with pink and blue leaves that looked like cotton candy. "We can make a tree house."

"The instructions are for a shelter on the ground," Selena pointed out.

"I've always wanted a tree house," Maya whispered. She had more dreams than she knew what to do with.

"I know what we can do!" said Eris with a big smile. "First we can build the shelter on the ground, and then we can fly it up into a tree!" She trotted off toward the clearing.

3
The Survival Challenge

The Melowies quickly got to work building their shelter. They followed the instructions exactly, without much talking. It was like they had been working together as a team forever. They gathered and cut sticks, tied them with ropes, and covered them with branches.

When they were done, they threw themselves down on the grass, exhausted but happy with their work. Their hut looked like an enchanted cube. It was a little bit of a tight squeeze, but all six of them fit inside.

"We didn't do too bad after all." Cleo laughed.

"There is no roof, though," Eris pointed out.

So they collected more branches and tied them like an umbrella to a pole, which they stood in the middle of the cube. Then they covered the top with pine branches.

"So how do we turn it into a tree house?" asked Maya.

"Easy! We just put it up in a tree!" Cleo replied. The six Melowies grabbed a hold of the cube and started lifting it into the air. Suddenly . . .

CRAAAASH!

"Cora, what are you doing? Why did you drop it like that?" Electra cried.

"There was a branch sticking out. It was ruining my hairdo!"

Electra rolled her eyes. "We're just lucky it didn't break. Come on, let's try this again."

This time they lifted the whole shelter up onto the big branches of an oak tree. They made a floor by tying branches together with pieces of rope and nailing them down with wooden nails that Maya carved. But even after all their hard work, their tree house still tilted to the left.

"It isn't exactly stable," said Eris. She

loved to find something wrong with everything.

"How about we put a long stick in the ground under each corner to support it?" Electra suggested.

"That's a great idea!" Cleo agreed.

Once they felt the shelter was steady, they went inside. "Wow!" they all exclaimed when tiny blue lights started darting back and forth. "Those funny little bugs are better than a chandelier."

"There is no closet to hang our clothes, or anyplace for me to plug in my hair dryer. How will I dry my hair after my shower?" Cora complained.

"We have only one change of clothes, and there is no shower!" Cleo pointed out to her friend. "So problem solved!"

"How do we brush our teeth?"

"We can use the water from the creek," Selena suggested.

"Brush our teeth in the creek?" said Eris, disgusted. "That is a gross idea."

"Well, it will be more gross in the morning, when our breath makes the leaves fall off the trees," Cora said.

"Let's get our beds ready," said Selena. "Unless we want to sleep on top of these scratchy twigs."

"I bet we could make some really

comfortable beds from the moss and leaves here." Even in that wild and strange forest, Electra cheered everyone up, because she always saw the bright side of everything.

The six Melowies flew back down to the ground to gather up some of the leaves, which were as colorful as confetti. Back in the tree house, they made them into six soft mattresses side by side. They felt like the queens of their own castle.

4
An Evil Plan

"My stomach is rumbling!" Cora complained. "What is for dinner?"

"Hamburgers and fries?" Cleo joked.

"I think we still have some work to do before we can eat anything," Selena pointed out. "We don't exactly have a stove. We will need to come up with something."

With a flourish of their colorful wings, the Melowies flew down from their tree house again and took another look at the instructions Ms. Ariadne had given them. They used some sticks planted in the ground and a few big rocks arranged in a circle to make a simple stove. After all that work, they were hungry and exhausted.

"Now all we have to do is start a fire," said Cleo, looking a little worried.

"Easy!" Electra said, reaching for the instructions again. "It says here that we need to find a piece of flint, which is a small rock. Then we have to scratch something made of steel against it."

"I think our flashlights are made of steel!" Maya said.

The girls looked around for a piece of flint

under the bushes. They found some leaves to catch the sparks and started scratching at the stone with their flashlights. It took a while, but suddenly something started happening.

"Wow, look at that! Smoke!" Cora said.

A small spiral of smoke was coming from the leaves. Then there was a tiny flame. They put the leaves under some dry twigs in their fireplace. It took a little while before it all caught, but they soon had a blazing fire ready to cook their dinner.

"Great, I will go and look for some plants that we can cook!" Maya exclaimed. "I'll get wild mallow, chicory, chard, and wild asparagus. I love vegetables! You'll see. Dinner is going to be delicious."

"My mouth is already watering," Eris snarled sarcastically.

"Did anyone happen to bring a sandwich?" whispered Electra. "Or some chocolate? I can't stand vegetables."

"So you can't stand food that's good for you?" said Maya.

"No, it's just that . . ."

"I will cook you a dinner that will make you feel fantastic, Electra! Trust me. Three pounds of nettle soup and two pounds of daisies in sap sauce with pine needles on top. Then, for breakfast, a cup of oak bark tea with—Electra? Are you okay?"

Electra had thrown herself on the ground, pretending to pass out. Right before she hit the ground, something caught her eye. Just inside the entrance to a cave not far away, there was something almost glowing on a rock. It was white and huge. It was a great big delicious egg!

"Hey, Electra, stop!" everyone yelled at the same time as Electra dashed over to the shiny egg. "That looks like a vulture cave. It might be dangerous!"

But it was too late; Electra had already disappeared into the cave.

"Electra, where are you?" Her friends called for her several times, but there was no answer.

"Where is she? What could have happened?" Cleo asked anxiously.

Cora gathered up all her courage and announced, "Let's go look for her."

The Melowies carefully walked into the cave, but Electra was nowhere to be seen. Neither was the egg. They could see another opening at the other end of the cave.

"She must have gone out through there," said Selena. "But why isn't she answering us?"

"Hey, look at that!" Maya said. When the filly got to the middle of the cave, she saw that there was more than one opening. There were five, each leading in a different direction.

"They look like the points of a star," Selena noticed.

"Let's split up," Cora said, taking control

of the situation again. "If we each take a different exit, one of us is bound to find Electra. We can mark our paths through the forest by making arrows with sticks on the ground. That way we can find our way back."

None of them noticed the sneaky smile on Eris's face. She had an evil idea. She had worked out how to pass the survival challenge and make the others look bad. She just needed to wait for the right moment.

Cleo, Maya, and Cora each took a different exit and walked deeper and deeper into the forest. Eris waited in the shadows of the cave and secretly followed Selena.

5
Dark Paths

Selena walked into the forest, calling Electra's name; her voice was mixed in with the voices of the other Melowies and a single owl hooting. There was no trace of Electra.

Suddenly, the glow of the plants around Selena faded. She didn't want to admit it, but she was scared. The only source of light was the tiny insects and their glowing blue antennae. What if she came across some scary animal hiding behind a tree, ready to eat her?

"Cora did have a good idea," she whispered to herself as she made another arrow on the ground with sticks.

Sometime later, the Melowy from the Night Realm sat down on a rock, feeling very tired and discouraged. She was so worried about Electra that she was about to cry. She looked back at the path she had taken and noticed that the arrows she had been making were gone! They had all disappeared, swallowed by the darkness, just like Electra.

Then Selena really did begin to cry.

"Electra, where are you? And what has happened to my arrows? How will I ever find my way back to the other girls?"

She sat and thought about a solution to her problem, but that only made her feel more trapped in this maze. There seemed to be no way out. But then she looked up at the sky. Thousands of stars formed constellations she had never seen before. They seemed to be showing her the way. The Power of Night had come to her rescue! She couldn't say how, but somehow she knew the stars were pointing her back to the tree house. She just had to let them guide her.

*   *   *

"This trail is all bends and curves!" Maya exclaimed. She had been looking for Electra everywhere but hadn't found a trace of her. Just as it happened to Selena, she was starting to feel alone and scared. She was not made for adventures. She missed her friend, who was the life and soul of their group, and the only one who could always cheer everyone up.

A thousand thoughts filled Maya's head as she bent down to make another stick arrow on the ground. "What if an animal comes and moves my arrows?" she wondered. "Or what if the wind blows them away? Maybe there should be a backup plan, just in case, some other way to find my way back. It's better to be safe than sorry."

She pulled a roll of gauze out of her survival backpack. She cut a few strips and tied them to the trees as she walked along.

A short time later, Maya finally gave up. *Electra couldn't have gone this far. Maybe she went back and is waiting for us at the tree house,* she thought. She turned around toward the tree house and realized her arrows had gone missing. She followed the strips instead. She still felt uneasy, though. After all, who had taken the arrows? And where had Electra gone?

6
Glowing Amber Eyes

When Cleo realized her arrows had all disappeared, she leaned up against a tree and sighed. She had no idea what to do next.

"What on earth could have happened to my arrows?" she wondered out loud. "I made so many of them. If only I could use some magic. But I don't even know what realm I come from, or what that magic would be."

Just then she heard a noise from nearby in the forest. It seemed to be coming closer.

Suddenly, two amber eyes appeared in the darkness, staring straight at her.

The Melowy held her breath as a wild boar with steam streaming out of its nostrils slowly walked toward her. It was a big brown boar, with stubby, chipped teeth. It

kept jerking its head back and forth as if it was getting ready to attack.

Cleo was so scared she couldn't move a muscle. She couldn't even think properly.

"Why haven't you jumped on me?" she whispered to the creature. "Do you enjoy scaring your food?"

Then she noticed the boar wasn't really jerking its head back and forth. It looked more like it was trying to point toward something. It even began pawing the ground with one of its powerful front legs. All of a sudden, the animal turned and started walking down a path. It looked back at Cleo and jerked its head again.

Cleo didn't know where she found the courage, but she finally dared to look the boar right in the eyes. The amber glow that had only a moment ago filled her with fear now seemed sweeter than honey. Her instincts told her to follow this odd creature. She could sense that it wasn't trying to hurt her; it was only trying to help her.

She walked side by side with the boar and eventually started to hear the sound of rushing water. The boar had led her back to the brook they found earlier. She was so excited to be back she almost didn't realize someone was kneeling on the path in front of her, brushing away arrows. She peered a little closer to get a better look. Just then, she heard another voice calling from the distance.

*　　*　　*

"Cleo!"

"Cora!" Cleo turned, looking around for her friend.

"Somehow all the arrows I left along the way disappeared!" Cora called as she bobbed along in the freezing-cold stream. She was letting the current of the brook carry her

back in the direction of the tree house. "While I was looking for Electra, I found a waterfall," Cora explained. "I went over for a drink, slipped on a stone, and fell in! Once again, the cold water saved me."

Cleo smiled back at her friend. But it wasn't really a happy smile. There was still no sign of Electra.

7
Free Fall

The moment she picked up the egg, a mysterious force sucked Electra farther into the cave. Next, the ground suddenly opened under her feet, and she felt herself falling. At first, she screamed, but then she noticed that she was falling very slowly. It was like she was in a dream.

When she finally landed, it was on something that felt like a soft mattress. It was completely dark, and darkness weakens

any Melowy from the Day Realm. Electra was a little scared, but she tried to look at the bright side. At least she was alive!

She could still hear her friends' voices in her mind. *Electra, stop! It might be dangerous!* Why hadn't she listened to them? Why didn't she ever think before acting?

All of a sudden, Electra heard a noise

nearby, and she froze in her spot. What if she had fallen into a monster's cave and it was coming to find her?

She couldn't see anything in the dark, but she heard what sounded like a door squeaking open in the wall behind her. She couldn't see the figure that appeared in the doorway, but she did recognize the voice.

"Hello, Electra."

"Congratulations, you are all right on time. It's ten o'clock, and here you are . . . Well, most of you, at least," Ms. Ariadne said, standing in the clearing under the tree house. She had come to take all the Melowies back to the Castle of Destiny.

"What a nice tree house," she said. "I see you didn't waste too much time making it attractive, though. Anyway, it's time to go back to school. Follow me!"

No one noticed the look on Eris's face. She seemed very surprised to see that the others had made it back to the tree house on time. The rest of the Melowies stared up at the tree house. Everyone else's shelter had been built on the ground. They all pointed and looked amazed. Maya, Cora, Cleo, and Selena didn't notice. They were looking down at the ground with sad expressions.

"What's wrong, girls?" Ms. Ariadne asked, seeing the looks on their faces.

"Well, one of our best friends is missing," Selena said.

"Yes, I noticed that. Oh well. You will just have to get used to life without her. When the going gets tough, the tough get going. Weaklings like your friend Henrietta, on the other hand, they get lost. The Castle of Destiny wants only the best students."

"Electra is not a weakling!" protested Maya, who was usually very quiet. This time, she could not help herself.

"Come on, there is no point in crying over her. Your friend failed the test—she didn't pass the challenge. You'll be better off without her. The principal is waiting for you. If you don't make it back, you'll be losers, too."

But the four girls did not budge. They weren't going anywhere without Electra, even if it meant they were going to fail the test. They all knew that any student who disobeyed a teacher at the Castle of Destiny would be expelled, but they couldn't leave without Electra.

8
A Test of Friendship

Eris was the only Melowy from the group who followed Ms. Ariadne.

"I have passed the test, and I don't want to get in trouble just because one of my group failed," she said. "You are right, Ms. Ariadne. Electra was weak and would never have made it. I'm coming with you. I will do anything to stay at the Castle of Destiny."

"That's the spirit," Ms. Ariadne said.

Now Cleo couldn't stop herself. She stepped forward, full of anger.

"Eris, I saw you last night, you know!" she shouted.

Eris stopped in her tracks as if something had bitten her. The teacher stopped as well.

"Of course you did!" Eris said. "We all wasted last night looking for Electra."

"We did, because she is our friend," Cleo said. "Only you weren't looking for Electra, were you? You followed each of us and threw away the marks we were making on the ground so that we couldn't find our ways back to the tree house."

"That isn't true!" Eris shrieked. "You are lying because you want me to fail like the rest of you."

The other Melowies stared at one another in amazement. "So that's what happened to our arrows!" said Selena. "That's okay—the stars showed me the way back."

"Luckily the stream carried me back," Cora said. "Otherwise, I would still be lost in the woods, too."

"I only found my way back because I tied bits of gauze to the branches as I passed," Maya added.

"And I met a boar that showed me the way!" said Cleo.

"If only something like that could have happened to Electra," Selena said. "Why couldn't she find her way back to the tree house? Maybe she is hurt. Maybe she has fallen somewhere."

"I know where she is," Ms. Ariadne interrupted, tipping her cowboy hat. "Follow me."

This time the Melowies trotted quickly behind the teacher. They were absolutely delighted to find Electra waiting for them at the gate of the castle. The four girls gave her a group hug.

"Electra!" Maya cried. "It's so good to see you again. We were so worried about you! What happened?"

"It seems this was part of the plan all along," Electra explained. "Ms. Ariadne wanted to see if we would be sensible enough not to put ourselves or the group in danger.

She placed the egg at the entrance of the cave to test us. Even though you all told me not to, I couldn't help myself. When I touched the egg, I began to fall down a hole. Principal Gia met me and brought me back here and . . . I know I was wrong . . ."

"Electra," said Ms. Ariadne. All the girls looked at her in shock that she remembered the correct name. "You're wrong now. Don't you remember what the instructions said? 'The biggest mistake is being afraid to make mistakes.' Your mistake ended up proving the strength of your friendship. You, Selena, Cleo, Cora, and Maya have passed the test— the test of friendship!

"That does not, however, apply to you," added the teacher, turning to Eris. Eris looked back at her with a gloomy expression. "I am going to make sure that your punishment will serve as an example for every student. You have shown that you care more about yourself than others, so your punishment will show you how to be caring. Theodora, the castle's cook, always has a lot of work to do. There simply isn't enough staff in the kitchen to help her. You will go down there to help her with the cooking and cleaning every day."

Eris rolled her green eyes. She couldn't stand the idea of helping anyone, let alone Theodora, with her honey-sweet manner and that annoying little dog. It was going to be hard for her to make it through this punishment.

In a secret room, Principal Gia was looking out the window, watching the sea of magical clouds that swirled around the Castle of Destiny. Then she turned and stared at the wall. Her face was glowing. "Maybe it's them," she whispered. "Maybe they're the ones who can save us!"

There was no one in the room with her. Just something that glittered in a strange and extraordinary way.

"There are evil forces who even now await their chance to destroy the balance," came a voice from the object. And Principal Gia knew that if those forces ever found out where the diamond was hidden, they'd stop at nothing to steal it.

Read on for a sneak peek of the next exciting moment in the Melowies' journey:

The Ice Enchantment

A Magical Morning

It was a beautiful, warm morning at the Castle of Destiny. The gentle breeze blowing off the sea of clouds made the air fresh and fragrant. It was an excellent start to a new day.

"Ew!" Maya cried. Her usually perfect mane was a complete mess. It was time to get out of bed, but she still had her blanket pulled right up to her nose.

"What are you ewwing about?" asked Cora, who was always up first. She was already dressed and her mane was styled beautifully.

"Today is our first Art of Powers class," Maya groaned, burying herself even deeper under the covers. "Don't tell me you've forgotten."

"Of course I haven't forgotten!" cried

Cora. "I'm so excited. I can hardly wait for it to start!"

"Lucky you. I'm terrified!" Maya muttered, finally sitting up in bed. "I'm so nervous that I didn't sleep at all last night."

Selena groaned and stretched. She hadn't slept very well, either.

Art of Powers class was very important for Melowies. Not only because it was something they had been dreaming about since they were little fillies, but also because they couldn't become true Melowies unless they learned to use their powers properly. Getting a bad grade in Art of Powers meant being expelled from the Castle of Destiny.

Electra yawned loudly. She had slept like a log and had only just woken up. She lay with her head hanging off the side of the bed, and her tail rested on her pillow.

"You'd better get a move on, sleepyhead," cried Cora. "You don't want to be late today!"

"Why? What is so special about today?" Electra mumbled, rubbing sleep out of her eyes.

"It's the first day of Art of Powers class," sighed Selena. "As if we don't have enough schoolwork already . . . I still haven't gotten over our survival challenge in the Neon Forest."

"But we all did really well!" said Electra. "Even though I went off after that egg. This class is going to be great. I can feel it. I already know how to use my power a little.

I realized that the other day." Electra winked at her friends and concentrated hard. Her face turned orange and was hot to the touch. Melowies from the Day Realm, like her, were connected with the sun's energy and light.

"Are you sure you know what you're doing?" Selena asked. "You look like you're going to burst into flames."

Electra was getting hotter and hotter. Sparks started to fly off her mane.

"No problem! Everything is fine! Don't panic . . . but I can't seem to stop it!" Electra cried, waving her arms to cool herself down.

EXPLORE DESTINY WITH THE MELOWIES AS THEY DISCOVER THEIR MAGICAL POWERS!

Hidden somewhere beyond the highest clouds is the Castle of Destiny, a school for very special students. They're the Melowies, young pegasuses born with a symbol on their wings and a hidden magical power. And the time destined for them to meet has now arrived.